I am a working mother of three beautiful children: Mica — my diamond, Jeremiah — my sunshine, and Josiah — my star. My husband John — my heart. I love them all so deeply, and without their support this wouldn't be possible. My passion for writing, and for different styles of writing, has been with me for the longest time. From real life to fantasy, romance to thriller, I just can't stop.

This is a work of fiction. Names, characters, businesses, places, events and incidents are either the products of the author's imagination or used in a fictitious manner. Any resemblance to actual persons, living or dead, or actual events is purely coincidental.

Midnight Shopping

Trisha Caress

Midnight Shopping

Vanguard Press

VANGUARD PAPERBACK

© Copyright 2023
Trisha Caress

The right of Trisha Caress to be identified as author of
this work has been asserted by her in accordance with the
Copyright, Designs and Patents Act 1988.

All Rights Reserved

No reproduction, copy or transmission of this publication
may be made without written permission.
No paragraph of this publication may be reproduced,
copied or transmitted save with the written permission of the
publisher, or in accordance with the provisions
of the Copyright Act 1956 (as amended).

Any person who commits any unauthorised act in relation to
this publication may be liable to criminal
prosecution and civil claims for damages.

A CIP catalogue record for this title is
available from the British Library.

ISBN 978-1-80016-572-4

Vanguard Press is an imprint of
Pegasus Elliot Mackenzie Publishers Ltd.
www.pegasuspublishers.com

First Published in 2023

Vanguard Press
Sheraton House Castle Park
Cambridge England

Printed & Bound in Great Britain

I would like to dedicate this to my forever inspiration, my mother. She knew long before me that I would go forth and do everything I always wanted to do, it has just taken longer than expected, she is no longer with me in body but she will always be beside me in spirit; she was my hero and forever will be. My second inspiration, another person I would like to dedicate this book to, is my daughter, best friend and business partner, Mica. She encourages me to keep going, reminds me how much more I have to give, and that my ability to write knows no bounds. I will continue to write as this is my vocation.

Thank you to all the people in my life who have doubted me and believed in me. Equally both parties have pushed me to be stronger and to be the best version of myself, and for that I love you all.
Hiya, see ya, bye T x

Chapter 1

RODGER

My name is Rodger. I grew up in what I thought was a normal family. My mum, my dad and my twin brother, Joe. Although we were a happy family, it was obvious Joe was the favourite, it didn't matter to me as he wasn't just my brother, he was my best friend. Growing up Mum would buy us bags of sweets but he would always have one more than me, in our Christmas stocking he would have an extra toy. I did ask Mum why Santa left Joe an extra toy. "I have been just as good as him all year."

Her reply was, "Santa must have left it by accident." On our birthdays, Joe's cake would be decorated, mine had a lot less added to it. He would have new trainers, his were brand names and mine were not. I never said anything about those things I just lived with it.

As we were growing up we were mischievous, we got into trouble, quite a lot to be honest. We broke people's windows throwing stones, stealing from shops, I even killed a squirrel. Joe was horrified I did that. We got caught a few times, when Mum and Dad found out he would got a telling off, I got a beating from our dad. He knew how to get around them and they believed every single word.

This went on for years. I knew when I reached eighteen I would leave home. When I left, I met the girl of my dreams, I found a good job at a car factory, the money was fantastic, and, after saving for a little while, I was able to mortgage my own home. Joe, however, continued to live with Mum and Dad, in our old room. He would come around from time to time; he seemed to be pleased for me I did, however, catch him eyeing up my girlfriend, Jane. She would tell me she felt uncomfortable with him in the house but I dismissed it and said that he meant no harm, he's just plain Joe.

As the months went by, Joe was a frequent visitor even when I wasn't there. One day I left work early as I wasn't feeling too good. As I got home I saw his bike outside my house. I crept through the door and could hear noises coming from upstairs so I went up and there they were in my bed having sex. The rage in me exploded, that was the day something clicked in me. I almost killed my brother but I didn't care at all, she had to drag me off him. The look in her eyes, was that of sheer terror. She got him out of there and took him to hospital, she got in contact with our parents, and that was the day they cut me off and called the police.

I was sent down for one year. In that prison cell I thought of nothing but revenge. Each and every day I became the target of someone's sick fantasy, I was sodomised, spat at, bullied and beaten. I had a target on my back, I couldn't contemplate why. I kept myself to myself and was no trouble to anyone but seemingly not a single inmate liked me. Was it my face? Was it because I was quiet? Did I seem weak? What on earth could it be. I would get each and every one of you that hurt me and my Mum and Dad were first on my list, I hated them. They disowned me, they disowned me because of what I did to my brother, forgetting what he did to me. My brother broke up my home, my relationship, my life, yet they still blamed me. It brought me back to the one extra sweet or toy they gave him. I delved deep into all the great times we had together and all the laughter we shared. Dad used to put me on his shoulders and run with me, we would jump in puddles until I was wet through and muddy, and laugh about it until we got home and mum would shout at us, well more so him for letting me do it Going on holidays as a family, our first time on an aeroplane was to Disneyland. All those magical times, why did they start to hate me? I asked myself this all the time. Why? And when? Why was Joe there special one? We were twins, why did he sparkle more than me?

Anger grew in me.

Four more weeks to go then I was out. Each day dragged, and the other inmates knew my time in there was nearly over, the violence was reaching its peak

My last week was by far the worst if that was even possible.

Tuesday morning, and we were in main hall, some of us were watching tv, some playing cards and other games and the rest we playing pool. One of the guys, Dean was walking up the stairs, "Rodg come up here a sec, I've got some books that you might like."

I liked Dean he was one of the select few that didn't give me any shit, and spoke to me from time to time, I didn't hesitate to follow him, I trusted him, and reading was on the things that got through my time in here. As I neared the top of the stairs, an uneasy feeling came over me, my gut told me that I had fucked up massively, I turned to walk back down but Darren and Peter were making their way up, then I felt a hand on arm, it was Wesley "Fuck." I told myself, "This way" he said as he pushed me to his cell, as I stood in front of his door I saw three other guys in there, Carlos, Linden and Ricky, the smiles on their faces made me feel sick. "Please Wes, don't do th…" before I could finish my sentence I was thrown to the floor, Darren and Peter came in and Dean stood watch at the door.

They took turns on me, the one after rougher than the one before I lay there and took it, there was no point in fighting back or screaming tears filled my eyes, but I didn't let them fall, the sounds they made as they penetrated me, I drowned out, my mind cast back to my childhood and happy times with my girl, I would soon be home.

As the day of my exit arrived, I walked past every inmate who had hurt me, I stared them all down, my eyes dark and as dead as the night. "I will see you soon," I said with a smile. The tone of my voice, pleasant, yet chilling. some of them looked worried but the majority just laughed. yet still it felt good. Soon it would be my turn.

As I reached the door to freedom I took a deep breath, even though I was a free man, my mind wasn't free. I had all this anger inside of me and the revenge I wanted to take needed to be released. Only then would I be free.

As I got home it was damp cold, full of dust and cobwebs but in that moment I didn't care,. I was home. First thing, put the fire on, it's a coal and log fire. Thank God I had it, as the electric and gas were not on as no one has been here. I sat down for a moment and looked around the living room, what had been such a happy place, filled with laughter and love not so long ago was now an empty and cold space, no love, no laughter, just me.

I needed to get the gas and electric back on, but for now a pan of water on the fire will have to do, at least then I could keep myself decent, I had to go shopping.

Thank God Jane didn't empty any of my accounts, she still had some morals it seems, I had quite a bit of money in there too.

My van started after a few tries too, someone must be looking out for me.

I filled my van full of food and drink, as I wouldn't be going anywhere for a while.

It felt good to be home, but as I sat in my armchair I thought to myself and once again asked why was I the one? Everyone disliked me, what did I do to deserve it? I blame my parents, they planted a seed and they kept watering it through the years. I just didn't notice at the time. I knew they loved Joe more but I thought they loved me too, looking back I don't think they even liked me and still to this day I will never understand why.

I decided to go around to my mother and father's house to see how they were, and test the water after all they are my parents. I pulled up to the huge farmhouse, that I grew up in, nothing had changed, only the land around them which looked unkempt but my dad was old now so I can imagine it wasn't easy for him.

As I got to the front door, I felt a little anxious but still I knocked. Dad answered. "What the hell do you want?" he shouted.

"I just came to see how you both are."

My mother came to the door and she said exactly what Dad said but with venom on her tongue.,

"Mum, I just wanted to see you both and check in"

"Well you can check out and don't call me that, never darken our door again! Especially after what you did to your poor brother. Joe is just so lovely and the perfect son, Why couldn't you just be more like him?"

"Mum, I tried, I really did, and Joe wasn't lovely when he was sleeping with Jane, I was in love, I was happy…"

"You were always different, attention seeking and dramatic, crying at every little thing," she interrupted.

"We tried so hard to put on afront and show love and kindness to you so no one would think badly of us, but now you're grown you're on your own, to us you are dead! I don't have to pretend any more, you are our greatest disappointment Rodger." The door slammed shut in my face, without given the chance to say anything more. I walked away, head down, my heart well and truly broken. A defeated man.

Everything she had said to me, tears washed my face.

I don't know what I did differently from my brother, as far as I am concerned we did most if not all things the same. We played together, got into childish trouble together, as youngsters we were best friends. Yes he was spoiled more than me but I didn't let it show that it got to me, we were all fine as a family.

By the time I reached home the tears had stopped, and rage engulfed my whole body. I grabbed a glass and the bottle of Jack Daniels I brought earlier, as I sat at my desk I knew now for sure I had to make them pay. I had tried to make amends but now they will pay for not loving me. All I could think of was killing my mother My blood ran cold, I felt absolutely nothing. I just stared into space. They had taken the nice right out of me. I plotted how to kill my mother. I knew I couldn't look up ideas on the computer as I have seen on films how the authorities can trace anything I look at, so it would have to be planned out on paper then burnt. I can't go and see them again as they don't want me around. I could wait for her to leave the house and slit her throat, the I know I'll just shoot her from afar, well I would if I had a gun, fuck's sake.

Tiredness just washed over me, I lay on the sofa but my eyes wouldn't close. Poison. I got straight up and went to the cupboard underneath the sink. Antibacterial wipes, rubber gloves and rat poison, bingo! My mother will die soon.

She became his first victim.

Chapter 2

REVENGE

Rodger had a rough idea in his head about how he was going to do this. He was hoping his mum still had the same car, although he couldn't remember seeing it the other day when he went round. He still had the spare key for it from when he used it once or twice, a few years ago, he knew his parents were sticklers for routine and would never get rid of anything that was still able and working.

In the dark of the night, he drove to his parents' house. Questioning himself the whole way, 'What the fuck am I doing? I am actually going to kill my parents? Can I really do this? How did I let myself get consumed with all this anger and hate?' As he drew closer to the house he decided to park down the lane and darken up, he pulled his hood up and used an old scarf to cover his face He sat for at least half an hour, his heart beating so fast and so hard, as though it could be heard a mile away. Holding onto the steering wheel his grip made his knuckles white as snow. Putting his hand on the door handle. He slowly pulled it open then closed it again. "Come on," he said to himself. He opened the door again then remembered. "Shit put your gloves on." He whispered to himself. Reaching for his backpack he checked he had everything he needed: rat poison, which he now had in a syringe filled to the top, check; no odour antibacterial wipes, check; some paper towels, check; and most importantly the keys to her car, check. "Right, I am ready!"

This time he got out of the car and looked around. The night was silently quiet, not a single person around. As he walked down the lane, a car came out of nowhere, with a loud roar. It scared the life out of him, he almost turned back, his heart pumping so hard it almost fell out of his chest. He took some deep breaths and proceeded to walk towards his parents' house. It came as no surprise that they still had the same car. It was right there in front of him, they never knew he still the key, which also had their house key on it, bonus. He didn't quite know what he was going to do with the poison just yet. but as he opened the car door straight away he spotted unopened water bottle in the holder. He thought he could deposit it in there.

'I can't open the bottle,' he thought, so he got the syringe out and, right at the neck of the bottle, he injected the poison, saving some in case he found something else, then put it back in its place and the syringe back in the backpack. He cleaned every bit he touched and got out of the car, cleaning the door handle even though he was wearing gloves. He looked at the house and couldn't resist putting the key in the door; he went in. It smelt just like it always did, Dad's stale fags, and musty. Rodger went into the kitchen and there was a cake on the side, she must have made it that evening as it was still warm. He cut a slice and just sat in the kitchen. After finishing the cake he crept upstairs.

Each step felt like the staircase would never end. As he reached the top he felt frozen, but his parents' bedroom drew him towards them almost like he was floating, like his feet didn't touch the ground. At the foot of the bed he stood, arms folded, it felt like a prompter was in front of him, all the vile words they have ever said and done appeared in front of him. "I truly hate these people, these people I had to call parents and now I know they hated me, they hated me for being born," he said to himself. He turned on his heel and walked down the stairs almost forgetting he needed to be quiet, went straight to the kitchen and injected the rest of the poison in the kettle, knowing that his mother like clockwork would be making a cuppa in the morning for them both, As he opened the front door he looked back one last time into the house that he grew up in and smiled. "Good riddance."

As he drove home, a calm came over him, and once back home, he got out of his clothes and got himself into bed. He slept like a baby that night.

The next morning he woke up, made himself a full breakfast on the fire and read his delivered paper just as if nothing happened, all the events of the night before forgotten; his heart had no feelings, no feelings for anything or anyone.

Days passed, he paced the floors, and wandered around aimlessly waiting, waiting to hear that his mother was no longer here. The wait eventually became unbearable, so he decided to get into his car and drove past his parents' house. The car wasn't on the drive, so he drove back home and collected his fishing gear, he needed to keep a clear head. As he was approaching his house, who was standing there, no other than his brother Joe. He took a deep breath then another, he was hoping this was the moment he was waiting for, the moment he would hear that their mum was dead. He took another deep breath and stepped out the car.

"Joe what the fuck are you doing here? I told you never to darken my door again!" He sounded just like his mother and wondered if he had become just like her.

"I am in trouble, Rodger, I had a fight in a bar last night and I knifed the bloke in his face," he replied, his tone clearly worried.

"What the hell has that got to do with me?"

"Bro!" he said. "I need your help!"

"Joe, fuck off from my front door! You're on your own, go and tell someone who cares, I am sure Mum and Dad will cover for you. I told you I would never forgive you for all the shit you put on me, all my life I thought you were the only one I could count on yet when I came home from work your in bed with my girl, you stole Jane, my twin brother, my best friend, and the last hope of human kindness I had, so I hope you suffer like I am doing. Where were you when I was inside? Why didn't you come and see me? I'm wasting my time! Look at you, you're pathetic! Now fuck off! You are no longer my brother and you mean nothing to me!" Rodger went into the house and closed the door behind him. Joe banged on the door for several minutes but to no avail. Rodger put some music on to drown him out and turned the volume up and opened a bottle of beer. The cold he felt for his brother was the cold he felt in his house and he knew one of them needed to be fixed. He still had no heating but he knew he had to keep the damp away, both from his feelings and his home.

He called the gas and electric company, they would arrive in the morning. Rodger took a glance out of the window, Joe was still outside sitting on the path, his head on his knees. A twinge of guilt came over Rodger but still he never gave in, keeping the curtains shut. "Joe will not feature in my life ever again," he told himself as he sat down on his sofa and, put his feet up, he closed his eyes. He must have fell asleep for a short while as he was awoken to banging on the door; it actually made him jump and he sat bolt upright. At first he didn't answer but it continued, so he answered the door.

"What the fuck Joe? I told you to go away!" he said, but it wasn't Joe, it was the police. "Why are you banging down my door like that? What the hell do you want?" Rodger asked.

"Mr Jones can we come in?" the officer said.

"Why?" he asked.

"Can we come in?" they asked again. "Mr Jones we need to tell you some bad news."

He let them in, "My name is not Mr Jones it's Rodger."

"Sit down Rodger," the female police officer said.

"I am fine where I am, what's going on?" Rodger replied.

She spoke with a soft voice. "Your parents were involved in a car accident, they didn't make it."

Rodger's face didn't change. "Why are you telling me?" he asked. "I don't care, they meant nothing to me!"

"They're your parents Rodger."

"Get the hell out of my house! They were Joe's parents! Go and tell him!" Rodger snapped back.

"Unfortunately, your brother was arrested earlier on today."

"And still I am not interested! Go away!"

As they were walking out the house she said, "We will be back tomorrow."

"Don't bother!" Rodger shouted. "I won't be in, just leave me be."

The next day arrived and, as they said they would, they were back. Rodger didn't answer the door. All day and during the evening, leaving roughly about two-hour intervals between each attempt, they kept coming so eventually he opened the door, and they just walked in. "Now sit down, Rodger!" PC Blake, as he introduced himself, barked.

Rodger did as he was told, but in his mind he was thinking, 'Did I get rid of all the evidence? Did I wipe the car clean?' A drip of sweat slid from his forehead but before anyone could notice he wiped it clean.

"Rodger, as we said your parents were involved in a car crash, your parents didn't make it and what the evidence tells us is that the actions of your mother caused the accident. She passed out while driving and your dad was in the passenger seat. They went head on into a Volvo carrying a family of four, all of which also died, there was also a lorry involved and the lorry driver is in critical condition and very lucky to be alive. It was a pile-up, a few other people got injured, so what we want to know is do you know of any health conditions your mother may have had that would explain why she passed out at the wheel? Can you shed any light on that, Rodger?"

"I know nothing about any of these people, yes, they were my parents, they made me but they never acknowledged me as their son, they told me a while back they never wanted or loved me. I went to see them after I came out of prison and they shut the door in my face, so you tell me if I know anything about her? And don't walk into MY house and bark at me telling me that *they're my parents and now they're dead,* what am I to do? Love them and care just because they're dead? Nothing has changed for me, I am glad they're gone."

"There will be an autopsy on your mother, Rodger, we shall let you know the outcome when it comes back to us," PC Blake replied, his voice gentle, as a sombre atmosphere filled the room.

Rodger began to panic. 'What if they found out it was me that poisoned that bitch?' he thought, whilst secretly feeling pleased that he had surpassed his intentions, never intending to kill two birds with one stone. Still he felt nothing, they were dead. PC Blake asked Rodger if he would like to see Joe.

"Do what you want as he's out of my life as well, I have no family." And with that the officers left and, when everyone had gone, Rodger had a bottle of beer, then another and so forth. He really didn't care for anyone or anything, the only thing he felt was elation for was what he had done, and the hunger to kill again. The thrill of it all was too exciting, being responsible for taking someone's life away. All night that's all he could think of and how his mother died. He was hoping she was crushed and her organs had splattered everywhere and that his dad was hopefully decapitated. He didn't care about the family of four who were stone cold dead, he had no cares. His heart turned black with pure evil, his eyes cold. He drank himself asleep on the chair around the dining table.

As the morning arrived he had vomited in his sleep, not even realising he had also urinated in his clothes. He stunk to high heaven but he didn't even wash, just changed his clothes to some other unwashed garments he had worn previously.

Rodger decided he wasn't going to do anything today, an engineer had come out to sort his gas and electric. "There you go Mr Jones, you can watch some tv now, and the hot water is back on." The engineer said, looking Rodger up and down.

"Yeah, thanks. Appreciate it" Rodger replied as he him out.

Walking back to his living room, he passed the mirror in the hallway and stood and looked at himself for a short while, he looked grubby, he needed a good wash, and he was starting to smell pretty awful, "oh fuck it!" he said out loud, and walked his arm chair, tv remote in hand, he sat back and switched the tv, it hadn't even been five minutes and there was a knock on the door, it was The police, he let them in. The stench of him and the clothes he had relieved himself in lay on the floor, the officers retched as they entered his home, still they had to do their job. "Rodger," PC Blake said. "Your mother's autopsy results came back, it turns out she was poisoned, according to her blood work, we believe it to be Rat poison. So this is now a murder investigation and we will need to speak to you again so don't go far. Everyone in your parents' circle are possible suspects."

Rodger began to perspire from his forehead, only this time the sweat came quicker than he could wipe it away. PC Blake must have noticed something was bothering him and asked him if he was okay, and that he seemed nervous,. Rodger replied, "Err… Yeah, I just have the flu, now get out of my house!"

The real truth was he was actually elated, the adrenalin pumped through his veins, he wanted to kill again. He imagined killing all the people that had ever hurt him in some way, pay back would be his bitch. That night he made a list of all these people and how long they had left inside. The list consisted of all the people in prison.

Wesley out in two weeks
Darren out in two weeks
Carlos ten years
Linden six months
Peter ten years
Ricky six months
Dean three months

"The only thing is, Carlos and Peter have got another ten years banged up, the others will be out in under six months," he said out loud. At least it would give him time to put his plans into action. He knew he couldn't do the same as he did to his mother as it wasn't as simple as that. He never dreamt he would kill anyone, this was brought on by the behaviour and attitude of others, and he just happened to thrive on it. His mind went into overdrive thinking of the things he would need. He knew his dad had a gun in his loft but how would he get into the house? The police could be watching the house, he would have to go in the dead of the night. Rodger figured that he would need chloroform, but he would make it from scratch, grip ties, tape, rope, cloth, and a face covering that would fit into everyday wear, it was a hat that turned into a balaclava, "perfect", he said to himself, so he wouldn't look out of place.

After having a few beers, he didn't know if he had slept, but morning soon appeared. Before having breakfast he took a trip down to the hardware store. People were gagging from the smell of him, and a little old man was brave enough to tell him so, "You need a bath mate!" Rodger looked around to see if anyone was looking, they weren't, so he punched that little old man square in the face and he fell to the ground.

Someone walked around the corner and Rodger bent down to him, acting as if he was concerned and whispered to him, "If you say it was me that hit you I will hunt you down and I will kill you." The old man was unconscious anyway. Rodger told the person that he just found him like that. The lady held her nose and told him she would go get help. Rodger got up, paid for his things and swiftly left. As he got home he swept everything off the table and placed everything he had bought on to it. He looked at it all admiringly. "Just a gun needed now, I will go to my parents' house tonight."

There was a knock at the door, it was the police again, their face masks were on them this time. "For fuck's sake!" Rodger huffed as he went to open the door, but they didn't come in this time.

"Just to let you know, Rodger, you are not a suspect in the underlying cause of your parents' death, as there is no evidence to say otherwise. We are still continuing with our investigation, but we just thought we would let you know, so you are free to go about your everyday life," PC Blake said.

"Well I could have told you that. How on earth would I? For a start I told you before they wanted nothing to do with me. I was dead to them," he said cockily with a sly grin.

"Well yes and from our calculations around the time the poison had to be administered into the body and given that your probation officer keeps tabs on you, we realised it couldn't possibly be you. We just wanted to let you know and thank you for your cooperation and we are sorry for your loss." And with that the officers left. As soon as Rodger shut the door, he let out a huge sigh of relief, realising that he had got away with it. These people would no longer be in his life although they weren't anyway but he would never bump into them on the street, see them at a function. These people were no longer. He hated his mother so much and now he hoped she would rot in hell, and as for his dad, well, all he did was listen and go along with everything that bitch of a mother said and did so he can rot too. They would be able to be buried soon, but Rodger would have no say or anything to do with it.

Chapter 3

NEW HOME

As the days and weeks passed by, the day had come for his parents to be buried. They had a basic funeral, as they didn't put much money aside for it, a funeral which was more than they deserved Rodger thought, plus Joe was locked up and had no money and Rodger would not be putting a penny towards it.

Joe begged him to go to the funeral, but Rodger was adamant he wasn't going, however, on the day and, with his sick mind, he decided to go. He wanted to see them being lowered into the dirt where they deserved to be. He didn't stand around their coffins, he stood far back so no one could see him, he was just there to make sure they were dead. As everyone left he went over to their graves and spat on them, then simply walked away.

A few days had passed when he got a phone call about their will from the solicitor, and arranged an appointment, luckily they had a slot for that afternoon.

Two p.m. soon arrived and Rodger had estimated it would take at least twenty-five minutes to get the solicitor's office; he needed to be there for two forty-five. He got to the office just in time, it was two forty and, as he made his way to reception he couldn't help but think what was left in the will for him. At the desk, before he could speak, the receptionist was retching from the stench coming from him, the same as everyone who came into contact with him seemed to do. She still kindly directed him to the office where the solicitor was waiting for him. Once in the office the solicitor spoke very quickly, not introducing herself just getting straight to the point, obviously wanting him to get him out of there as soon as possible. She told him his parents had left him the farmhouse and his brother everything else.

'Great,' he thought to himself, but showed no emotion to the solicitor. 'The will was done quite a few years back and knowing what I know now they probably would have changed it, if they weren't dead,' he told himself. He was handed the keys and he left.

Rodger went straight to his parents' house, well his farmhouse, and headed to the loft where his dad had a gun, but to his surprise there was more than one. Rodger was wondering why his dad would need all these and if he did, why leave them in the loft, there was quite a few things up there but he couldn't be bothered to look through it all, so he got what he wanted: guns and the ammunition too. He looked around the house, pictures of his parents and Joe everywhere he turned. "Was I wiped out of the family a long time ago and never realised?" He thought back to when he was a young boy and they went to the beach as a family. He would sit on the sand by himself while his parents and Joe would be building sandcastles together, far apart from him. It was as if he didn't belong, he never saw it, but it was all quite apparent now. He remembered how Joe would get a double ice cream cone, while he would only get a single. Anger raised up in Rodger and he smashed every picture in the house and burned them in the back garden. He could smell his dad's scent on the chair he had sat on for years. That went on the fire too but only after he had put his hands down the back to see if anything had dropped behind it, and he was glad he did, there was wads of cash stuffed down there. the flames grew higher, he wasn't worried about the neighbours though as they were miles apart. Now to go look in the old settee, exactly the same but so much more. There must have been fifteen grand or more. He decided to keep the settee as he needed somewhere to sit and sleep. It also didn't have either of their scents on it as his mother kept a throw over it, "Perfect!" he thought.

He laughed out loud. "They would be pissed that they didn't change the will, I got all their stashed money and this big old house life is a bitch. I never thought I would end up this way, but I'm fucking happy happier than I've been in a long time. Rodger you have won this race." he couldn't help but smile his luck had changed, "I am quids in! What do I spend it on? Do I split it with

Joe? No, fuck him, he doesn't need to know about the money, no one does and after all he is in prison, Ha Joe's in prison, i wonder if he disappointed mum and dad like I did? And just before they died too. Hopefully he gets treated the way I did in there. Prick!" Still with the house and the money it didn't fill the gap of the love they never gave him. He sat on the settee and counted all the money, forty-three thousand pounds. Some were old notes he couldn't spend but that was fine as it was only a few. "This is for the extra smacking you gave me, this is for hating me, this is for not loving me."

He had to go out for a walk and clear his head, it was dark outside too. 'Perfect,' he thought. He slipped his coat and gloves on and his balaclava, he walked for miles trying to get rid of his thoughts of everyone that had hurt him, his parents started it, but he still didn't understand why he was a target for everyone else. What was it about him that even a mother couldn't love? The happiness he felt earlier soon dispersed as it wasn't real, it wasn't enough. Tears built up in his eyes, he could barely see, but in the blur of his tears he saw a woman walking her dog. She looked just like his mother, the anger he was feeling towards her was all he could see: it was his mother, her face. As the woman got closer, the anger and adrenalin inside him grew, he couldn't help what he was about to do, he grabbed her round the neck and flung her on to the grass bank. He squeezed her neck so tightly that she was just about to pass out, until suddenly the black mist started to clear from his tear-filled eyes. He looked at the woman and saw it wasn't his dreaded mother. The woman's dog was snarling and was biting at his arm and legs, he kicked the dog so hard it fell on its side. He released his hands from the woman's neck, he thought he had killed her as she didn't scream, nothing came out of her mouth, or had he terrified her into silence? He felt no guilt as he walked away, he must only have walked twenty minutes, before turning on his heels, he was aroused at the thought of what he had just done. He had to release himself inside of her. He picked up his pace, but when he got back to the spot, there was no sign of her. He searched for a few minutes to no avail, so he pulled down his zipper, knelt to the floor and wanked himself off; it didn't take him long. He felt liberated, however, soon after realisation hit him. 'Shit! Shit! Shit! What if she recognised me?' he thought, while panic started to set in. He then remembered he had his balaclava on and he would have left no fingerprints as he had his gloves on. The only thing were his footprints and now his sperm. He kicked the mud where he had ejaculated trying to bury it with his foot. He thought tomorrow he would get some new boots, after all money is no object any more. The panic left him just as quickly as it arrived. Once he got home and still aroused from what had happened, he masturbated again while thinking about having his hand wrapped around that woman's neck wishing he had squeezed the life out of her. He held his penis so tightly that it almost turned blue. It gave him great pleasure.

Chapter 4

PEPPER AND THE PIGS

The time was now two o'clock in the morning, but he couldn't sleep. The silence of the night kept him awake, he could only sleep with noise around him and although he now lived on a farm, there were no animals. A light bulb moment appeared in his head, he decided he would have to get some pigs. He went on his parents' computer to see where and how he could purchase them and it just so happened one of the farms seven miles down the way had some for sale as the couple who owned them were getting too old to care for their animals. They had thirteen pigs, one of them pregnant, so he sent an email to purchase them and that he would pay in cash when they were delivered, as he didn't use credit or debit cards.

"Right that's sorted," he said, rather pleased with himself. Rodger then went and looked in the fridge, it was loaded with food, also the pantry was stocked with dried goods and tinned items. He wouldn't have to go food shopping for a while, and there were milk bottles at the front door so he assumed it would be delivered daily. He had a bite to eat, and soon the sun rise appeared, he was all of a sudden so tired from all that had gone on that he fell asleep on that rickety settee but compared to the bed in prison this was a dream, at least it was cushioned. But no matter what he slept on, his nightmares would haunt him constantly, he only managed to get an hour here and there, the very thing he needed, sleep, was the very thing that disturbed him, and it hurt. He decided in that moment he would try and sleep during the day, plus he would not have to interact with other human beings unless he chose to, the dark of the night would be his daytime. He didn't want to live like other people as they seemed to judge him from his appearance and instantly dislike him for just existing. Like with everything else in his world, Rodger had no cares, he had to be as cold as they were, that was only his thought process.

The weeks went by, his pigs had already arrived and settled in nicely. He put a lot of time and energy into them, he loved those pigs, like other people love their children. The pigs were loyal, they never spoke back, all he had to do was feed them. The pig that was pregnant when they first arrived had not long given birth. Sadly one of the piglets was rejected by her as it was a hard delivery, but Rodger thought that no matter how bad the birth was she still should have loved her, what made her different from the other piglets? It felt like how his mother had no love for him, it made him angry, he left her for 5 weeks so the others could feed off her and build their strength but eventually he killed that pig, slowly. Firstly chopping off its snout, then one leg at a time, next its tail, before finally ripping out its heart. He cut up the bits he could keep and put it in his freezer. "That will teach you bitch for abandoning your baby." Rodger felt accomplished, as if he had done some good for avenging this little piglet. He decided to hand rear the piglet, it wasn't a problem as he didn't sleep much anyway, only when his body and mind allowed and only during the day. Every two hours he would need to feed her and he called her Pepper as she was always sneezing.

Pepper lived in the house with him and, of course, she wasn't house trained but he didn't care, as he was becoming used to living in filth. When he was in prison he had to clean his cell but at home no one was on his back to do so, so he didn't. His parents would have been ashamed how their house looked apart from the upstairs which was pretty much the same as he didn't go up there, well that is he thought, he hadn't seen what Pepper had done up there, that was a different story, as she was allowed to venture everywhere in the house.

It was time for him to feed Pepper her milk, every two hours was a chore but he treated that little piglet like he should have been treated as a child. The news was on as usual, for him that was his company, that's all he watched and listened to in the background. What came on today, however, made him prick up his ears, the women he strangled was very much alive and well. Somehow she had managed to get to the nearby village;

he had hoped she had died on those hills as it was bloody freezing. According to the newsreader apparently when the police and ambulance were called the only words she muster were, *"The smell, the smell, the smell!"* And although weeks had passed she still remained saying those same words, *"The smell."*

"Cheeky bitch! And this is why I don't fuck with people during the day! So rude and judgmental!" Rodger spat at the telly. The chief of police was now on saying they've put out an alert and were welcoming anyone with any information to come forward and asking if anyone had seen anyone suspicious around the village. They had no clue where to go or look as the woman hadn't given any information apart from those words: *The smell*. They were frustrated but knew the woman had gone through so much trauma already that they couldn't push her any further, it would be a waiting game, and no one has come forward so far. Rodger was elated as he knew the more time that passed the more likely he was going to get away. Yet again.

Chapter 5

WHO'S NEXT?

Rodger decided that he would go out and find his next victim. This was no longer a whim, he couldn't not feel that pleasure, that satisfaction again, this was now a mission. Rodger needed his 'goodies as he liked to call them. He only had a limited supply here at the farmhouse. For what he wanted to do, he needed to go back to his place to get his goodie bag which still had the grip ties, tape, some poison, the syringes and his homemade chloroform plus some other bits in there, but right now he had some farm work to do

Once back inside his farmhouse, Rodger sat back on the rickety settee which was now filthy, still trying to comprehend how he had got away with the attack on that woman. He was thrilled to the point of bursting, which brought him to his next thought: his next victim and what he would do. Out of nowhere a tiny pang of guilt hit him. "What the hell am I doing? Planning to go out and kill somebody just because I feel like it, what am I becoming?" he asked himself. Those little moments of guilt were very quickly replaced with his own pain, and he very quickly remembered who he was and why he was like this, hatred built into every orifice of his being. Every person that had ever crossed him or crosses his path was going to feel his wrath and will meet the same fate as his parents. The men from prison were firmly on his list and, as he promised them all, they would see him again at some point. Waiting for some of them to be released would be long to wait, so he decided to check 'the list' to see how much longer it would be and, to his surprise and with all that was going on with the pigs and the house, he had forgotten that Wesley and Darren, two of the inmates and the first on his hit list had been released a few weeks back. The excitement started to rise in him but right now that would have to wait, he felt tired, realising he hadn't had any sleep that day. He tried to have a power nap, it was eight in the evening which was the time he would normally rise but with having Pepper everything had changed but now she was old enough so hopefully things could get back to normal. Whatever normal was.

Nothing was normal in Rodger's life, only in his dreams. The nightmares had now stopped for now and he dreamt of all the love and exciting things he did as a child, how much his parents doted on him and his brother equally, how his dad would throw him in the air and catch him as he fell back down in his adoring arms with the most loving and kind smile on his face, how his mother use to read him stories and how they used to laugh and how she would tuck him into bed like a sausage, with kisses on his forehead, leaving the room telling him she loved him. It was of course only a dream, in reality everything was very much the opposite. He woke a few hours later, dragging on whatever clothes he could find, buttered two slabs of bread and with whatever was in the fridge, slapped it between them, a quick swig of milk and off he went on one of his long walks only to remember he still needed to get his goodie bag. Nevertheless he carried on.

A mile down the road he spotted a couple in the distance who had two huge dogs, so he took a different path and carried on walking. He happened to stumble upon another farmhouse a few miles away from his. He crept up to the windows. As he got closer he fell to the ground, tripping over a hose; he hoped no one had heard him. Scrabbling to his feet he edged closer, holding onto the window ledge he peeped inside. He saw an old man in the kitchen sitting at his dining table. He watched that man while he ate, which seemed like forever. He was holding a cup of coffee now and he was trembling quite badly, he was clearly ill, maybe Parkinson's disease, he thought. Rodger stayed at that window for another hour making sure no one else was in that house, tonight wasn't the night he would kill.

Author: Sorry if I got your hopes up. I did, didn't I? You'll be hearing more from me later.

The thing was, as he didn't bring his bag of goodies, he didn't know how he could execute this killing without it. Rodger went back home. As he entered the door, Pepper had shit right on the mat. Rodger slipped and fell in it. Shit was all over his clothes, so he got a tea towel and quickly wiped himself down and that was it, tea towel back on kitchen side where he found it.

Author: Writing this book I cannot understand why he will not bathe or at least change his clothes. I simply cannot imagine how the stench of him wouldn't burn his own eyes. Rodger is a disgusting man with disgusting habits, his body will surely rot soon.

Chapter 6

LET IT BURN

Rodger walked back and forth. He just couldn't relax. So he decided to get in his car and drive to his place to collect his bag. Upon entering his house, it was so cold, the walls were mouldy, he knew he had nothing left there any more. He grabbed his bag and chucked it in the car, then he went into his garage to find a petrol can. He found it but it only had a little fuel left in it. He walked back into the house and straight into the kitchen and poured a little bit of the petrol onto the net curtains and the same in the living room and some on the carpet, lit a match in both rooms and threw them, thinking they would catch. He turned his back and walked out and closed the front door. Getting back into his car he drove off in the direction of the farm. He thought the fire would probably be a slow burner as he had only poured a little fuel, but good riddance, he didn't need or want anything in that pokey place, he had his farmhouse now, which was bought and paid for. His parents more than likely didn't want him to have it but, regardless, it was now his.

Once back in the farmhouse, Pepper had shit in the same place but this time Rodger saw it and just climbed over it. The house stunk to high heaven, but he couldn't smell it. He put the news on his TV and yet again, there was the same woman he had strangled, *'the smell'* woman as he now referred to her. Apparently she was so traumatised she remained in hospital and would be there for a considerable amount of time. The chief of police pleaded for any information, anything at all that could help. "This is of grave importance, we must find the assailant as he or she is highly dangerous, and at this moment I'm urging everyone to stay indoors after dark."

Rodger listened to everything, word for word, he didn't even flinch. "They would never think about me, I was covered from head to toe," he said.

Or so he hoped.

Author: Are you bloody stupid Rodger? You're getting complacent now, your Midnight shopping is all messy, if you want to continue what you're doing, think before you act. With your house, why did you try and burn it down? You have failed, by the way, as it was too damp and bloody cold, the matches blew out as soon as you threw them, you just didn't take any notice. Everything you do, you must have attention to detail. Also do yourself and everyone else a favour and have a bath, as you stink. I don't know why I had the audacity. Yes I know I am the author but I cannot change anything about him now and nor do I want too.

The time was now three thirty a.m., and Rodger had a moment of madness. He got into his car and drove back to the house he thought he had burnt down, which of course he hadn't. He felt a failure. He could hear his mother's voice and could see her face vividly as if she was standing in front of him. "You couldn't even burn down your own house, ha, ha, ha. You're not my son, you're a worthless, disappointment of a man and no one will ever love you." He rubbed his eyes to rid himself of her face but she was still there. "Look at you. You disgust me, you will be by yourself forever, you're unlovable, now get to your room!" In that very moment he felt like that little boy, he had forgotten how he was really treated, and all the bad memories started flooding back one by one. That's why he would wet himself and, as he stood now, he looked down to see himself in a puddle of urine. He rubbed his eyes once more, this time her face disappeared. He opened his living room door which was still as he left it. He was so angry that, after shutting the door behind him, he threw anything that wasn't screwed down, then he got himself a drink from the kitchen: whisky.

'Perfect!' he thought, and he drank half the bottle and slumped to the floor. Morning soon appeared and he realised he would have to stay until it got dark, so that's what he did, right there on the cold floor, still wet in his urine-soaked clothes. He had a knife in his hand, how it got there he had no idea, brushing against to and fro against the veins on his wrist, he continued drinking and started piercing his wrists with the knife. He felt nothing as the whisky had numbed whatever feelings he had, he passed out again at some point for several hours, only to be woken by people walking by the house. He felt the pain on his wrist and all the way up to his inner elbow, he wrapped his arm in some dirty cloth and drank his whisky, almost vomiting with every gulp. His life meant nothing to him but he was still alive like a cruel twist of fate. Nothing he did would let him be free from what his life was and continued to be.

Author: I do feel slightly bad for him. I didn't think he had wanted to take his own life, how wrong was I? Writing this has surprised me, Rodger's true feelings are buried so deep and now the roots are sprouting one by one, his mother is constantly in his thought, dreams and nightmares and it is his reasoning, his hatred for her surrounds his every thought process, and this is why not one human being is worthy to him.

Soaked in urine, vomit and pig shit he fell into a heap once again. He needed to go to the bathroom for a shit but he didn't make it. He soiled himself, and the smell of him surrounded the room and stuck to every bit of furniture like dust. He couldn't wait for night to fall, he had to get out of this house, the place he had called home for a short while. The house he now resided in was just as hellish but he was raised there not that that was any consolation but it all belonged to him and that was now his home. That bitch he called Mother would hate to know that he had it.

This peculiar day dragged on and on, it seemed like it was never ending, all he had was his thoughts, thoughts that a normal person wouldn't even conjure up in their nightmares. "God," he said. "I need to get out of here." He couldn't breathe, he opened the front door, not even knowing night had already fallen. He took a deep breath and then another but still he couldn't breathe, it took him quite a while to compose himself.

Rodger slumped into his car and just sat frozen to the seat, he wondered what was happening to him. 'Is this my time to die?' he thought as another panic attack approached him. He didn't want to die, so he took many deep breaths again. "Focus," he said to himself. "Focus you bastard." Hitting the steering wheel he repeated, "FUCKING FOCUS!" He revved up the car, screeched out of his drive through the country lanes. He put his foot down, getting up to the speeds of a hundred miles an hour, luckily his breathing was almost back to normal, he had to concentrate on his driving. "It's a good job no one else is on these lanes." The fuel was running low so he had to find a petrol station, he knew there was one nearby and he could just see it on the corner of the lanes. He filled up the tank and went to the booth to pay, but even through that small slit the cashier recoiled with the smell of him. He had shit himself earlier and pissed however many times now, what did he expect from people?

"Leave the money on the counter!" the cashier shouted. That pissed Rodger off, the rudeness of him. He chucked the money at the screen, notes and coins everywhere.

"There you fucking go, a please would have been nice!" Rodger snapped back. He didn't realise how awful he smelt.

Author: How the hell can he not know how badly he smells? He hasn't had a wash of any kind for god knows how long! It wasn't just his demeanour that people didn't like, the smell of him was much much worse and times that by 100.

Chapter 7

PERFECT TIMING

On his way home, tears dropped out of his dark seeded eyes, but he quickly wiped them away, as he didn't have any feelings after all. He arrived home but he didn't bother going into the house, he just walked and walked. He contemplated going back to the old man's house as he wanted to hurt someone, he was enraged, his hands shook with the wanting of putting them around someone's throat. He wanted to kill someone. Anyone. He wanted blood. He carried on walking for miles on end, pounding the streets, walking with his head down. To his astonishment he could hear footsteps coming towards him. 'Who the fuck is out at this time?' he thought. His head remained in the same position but his eyes rose up, then back down only to realise it was Wesley, one of the other men on his 'list'. He took another look, yes it was confirmed. Wesley was one of the inmates who had raped and beaten him in prison, he came out pretty much the same time as Darren, and

Darren was the first one he wanted but when life gives you lemons…

As Rodger and Wesley passed each other Wesley stepped aside. "Fucking hell! You stink!" Rodger didn't say a word, he just walked past, all the while knowing this would be Wesley's last night on earth. He pretended to walk into someone's garden as if it was his, only so he could turn around and follow Wesley. Rodger followed him for what seemed like forever but it was only thirty minutes or so. He entered a tall building of flats and began to climb the stairs. It had to be the top floor didn't it.

"As if I haven't walked for miles already," he told himself but knowing this would be worth it, he lingered behind Wesley taking each step carefully trying to make no sound. Luckily for him no one was around as it was normal people's hours of sleep. The mole on Wesley's face was prominent as he turned to the side looking around. Rodger had always wanted to rip it straight off his face, it would always stare at him when Wesley entered his cell. He watched as he took out his key and fondled the keyhole, then entered his flat. Rodger waited for five minutes, he took another look around to make sure no one was about, then he knocked on the door with a silent tap. No one answered, so he tried knocking again.

"Who is it?" Wesley shouted. Rodger remained silent so Wesley answered the door. "What the fuck do you want?" Rodger pushed hard against the door, as

Wesley with the full force of his body was trying to hold the door so he couldn't get in. But Rodger wanted this, he needed this. He pushed back harder, his weight behind it, and the door flung open sending Wesley crashing to the floor. "What the fuck do you want?" Wesley asked, trying to sound tough but the weakness in his voice was apparent. Rodger whacked him across the head as hard as he could, knocking him out clean. Grabbing him by his feet, he dragged him into the next room, the bathroom, he picked up the top half of his body, as heavy as he was he managed it, and threw his head to the bathroom sink. *Clunk*. Wesley's front teeth scattered like Tic Tacs on the tiles of the floor, blood pouring from his mouth.

Rodger left him on the floor along with his teeth to find anything he could to tie him up. The kitchen and living room were combined and everywhere was clean and in place, pretty much how their prison cells would be. He went into the kitchen and searched each drawer, he found the sharpest knife and some scissors, a drill which was under the sink along with some unopened duct tape. Into the fridge he went, there was beer and lots of it, he took a can and had a big gulp then spotted a loaf of unsliced bread, he ate the lot not realising how hungry he was, and realised he hadn't eaten all day. He grabbed the knife and the other things he had found and entered the living area that's when he clocked the curtain ties, he took them off so he could use them to tie Wesley's hands and feet, who, back in the bathroom, was still out cold. Rodger put some tape across his mouth and wrapped it around the back of his head twice, tied his feet together and tied his hands in front of him. Rodger went back to the kitchen to get his can of beer and grabbed a few more out of the fridge. He sat on Wesley's sofa as if it was his own, and drank one beer after the other. He thought to himself, 'Let me go and tie his hands behind his back, just in case.' With Wesley still out cold in the bathroom he undid the curtain tie, turned him over and tied them so tight that Wesley's hands were blue. Back on the sofa, more beer, Wesley had really stocked up, he was probably going to lay low as well. Rodger could barely keep his eyes open. He gave up in the end, he knew Wesley wasn't going anywhere as the door was bolted and the heavy chest of drawers he had taken out of the bedroom was against it.

Author: Sorry guys I forgot to tell you Rodger had done this, I cannot remember everything, it simply slipped my mind. Right back to it.

Rodger fell into a deep sleep, his nightmares back, they engulfed him. "No one will ever love you!" He was raped all over again and he felt every inch of his insides being ripped apart. He was in pain, the same pain he endured on a daily basis back in prison. It was happening now at that very moment, on that very sofa where he lay, he twisted and turned, he cried out in sheer terror. "Never darken my door again! You were never loved by me! We never wanted you!" He felt instruments entering his behind, he heard, "Chuck the money on the counter!" He saw himself sitting on the bench while his mum and dad and brother played happy families, every horror, every piercing word, and his mother's voice, all of everything joined together in that nightmare. "I wish I had never had you, you're worthless, what are you doing at my door? What do you want?"

Her voice jolted him awake, he bolted up and got to his feet, anger and rage roared through him. Like a hound chasing a fox, he headed to the bathroom where Wesley lay. He writhed and wriggled in pain. Rodger pulled him by his feet to the living room, the knife he had found earlier appeared in his hand, he didn't know what he was going to do with it. The mole on Wesley's face stared at him, remembering how that bastard behind that mole had raped him, he was going pay. First that mole needed to go. He put the knife to Wesley's face and proceeded to slice it, it proved much harder than he thought as the knife wasn't the sharpest at all. Nevertheless he dug into the flesh surrounding it, Wesley kept wriggling with the pain it was causing. Rodger put the knife to Wesley's throat, he couldn't scream as he still had the duct tape doubled securely around his mouth. Rodger dug deep into the flesh again, the knife ripped into his skin surrounding the mole. This time it was successful, the mole and flesh were finally removed. Blood poured out like water from a tap, so he took off Wesley's sock and stuffed it into the small hole he had created in his face. He then proceeded with the scissors, cutting off the flesh around the now removed mole, he then carefully placed the mole and flesh on the coffee table beside him. He looked at Wesley whinging on the floor. "How does it feel you fucking bastard? Are you hurting yet? I don't think you are hurting enough!" The evil in Rodger's eyes, so cold, yet so driven. Next he cut off Wesley's penis. "You won't be able to do any damage with that now will you?" He then turned Wesley onto his front and put a slit in his jeans at his rear leaving his bare backside facing up. He went into the kitchen and started rifling through the drawers, where he found a rolling pin. "This will do!" he said and went back over to Wes. He shoved the rolling pin right up his ass. "How does it feel to have something rammed up your arse that you didn't want?" Whilst he thrust that rolling pin back and forth, Wesley was trying to scream under the duct tape. Rodger continued to do this until his arm got tired. Blood poured from Wesley's backside. He removed the other sock and stuffed it in his ass.

He turned him over and said to him, "This is what you and your cell mates did to me every day, taking it in turns, now how does it feel you mother fucker?" Rodger stabbed him in his eye. "Answer me you bastard!" Before he knew it, he had stabbed him hundreds of times, he was dead but that wasn't enough. He continued, he needed to do this for himself, so he cut out Wesley's eyeball and placed it on top of the mole. "Now you can forever see that mole like I had to every fucking time you raped and sodomised me. I hope you rot in hell."

He cleaned his boots, washed his hands and wiped down and cleaned every surface he could remember touching hoping not to leave a trace, luckily the sofa was covered in some sort of plastic. Wesley for everything that he was, was also a clean freak, which worked in Rodger's favour, he ripped the covering off and folded it up so he could take it with him. As he was about to leave he looked back at the damage he had done. He had no care for Wesley, no one would miss him and no one would notice that he wasn't around. No one cared for a criminal like him. Rodger smiled and left and took the long walk home. The release he felt was intense, he was satisfied. For now.

Chapter 8

A HAPPY PLACE

One cell mate down, he would get the rest eventually.

As he arrived home, Pepper had left him a welcome home shit. "Thanks for that!" he said. He decided that tomorrow Pepper would join the rest of the pigs in the pen, he half-heartedly cleaned the shit up, as it was becoming wedged in the door. He got the shovel and wheelbarrow from the shed. He picked up so much shit, the wheelbarrow was nearly full, it was shocking for the short amount of time he had been living there. In the shed, there were some jars with lids, he put shit in each and every one of them, there must have been a dozen or so. What he was going to do with them he didn't know, he just thought he would keep them, so he did.

He left the wheelbarrow and shovel outside the back door, and went back into the house. Most of the house was scattered with shit and piss, both his and Pepper's. The only bit of the house downstairs that was completely missed was the cloakroom underneath the stairs; his mother would put him in that space for hours on end. For Rodger it would be his happy place, Joe would sneak in small toys and a small blanket as she would strip him to his pants. When his parents were not looking, Joe would bring him water and slices of dry bread or a biscuit. What she thought was punishment to him actually wasn't, he would talk and play with his Action Man and little cars without a care in the world. At least he wasn't being shouted at or being belted or slapped for no reason other than being born. So many memories kept coming back to the surface. He had buried so much deep down, all the things she had done to him as a child, that sometimes as an adult he would cry but silently.

Rodger opened the door to that cupboard, there was a hoover and a few more cleaning things. Rodger removed them, he also removed his clothes, well, peeled them off leaving them outside the door. The shit he had in his pants fell to the ground. He got into that happy place. It was really small to him, now he was a man, as a child it was huge but, nevertheless as soon as he crouched down he felt safe. In the corner was still his Action Man and the car he used to play with. It brought tears to his eyes as he then realised that was the only time he was truly happy. Those tears got bigger and he cried out, "Why did you hate me? What did I do? Why Mummy?" His mind went back to Joe, if it wasn't for him maybe I would have starved to death or died of thirst. "Maybe I should forgive him." But he couldn't as he had stolen the only happiness he had found. "No! He stole my girl he knew how much I loved her!" He couldn't forget that. Rodger started to get cold so he got a blanket and stayed in that room for the rest of the night.

The night soon fell into day. The cupboard was in complete darkness when the door was shut, the only light shone through the gaps at the top and bottom of door. That was enough as a child and enough now. Sucking back

those tears, he thought 'That bitch isn't worth it.' She haunted his dreams, turned them into nightmares, so he would not let her into his happy place. He wished he could kill her all over again, he would slice her limb from limb, starting with her tongue. He hoped she rots along with everyone he kills in hell, he wished her eyes had been gouged out by the biggest ugliest worm. He knew that bitch was dead and none of the above would affect her but that didn't stop him from wanting it to be true. It angered him so much when the police told him that his parents probably felt no pain. He was vexed to the core, so vexed he got out of his safe place as it wasn't where he wanted to be angry. Once out he shook the rest of the shit out of his trousers, pulled them back on with the rest of his clothes. He knew he needed to go out and get some supplies, as much as he didn't want to, he hated going out mixing with the public but he needed fresh food. He couldn't just live on tinned food alone, he needed milk as it was no longer delivered, he wanted bread, potatoes, veg, fruit and especially beer, lots of beer and a few bottles of the harder stuff, whisky, brandy etc. He always tried to stay away from people and would love to be able to order online as he hated the thought of going to a supermarket. It gave him anxiety, everyone stared at him and would avoid him like the plague, but he had no debit or credit cards, so he had no choice.

Author: Rodger people stare at you because of the state you are in and the reason why they avoided you is because you stink very badly, all you need to do is have a bath from time to time and wash your clothes, better still go and get new ones and burn the ones you're wearing. Just saying!

He dragged on his coat, everything he wore was so crusty and the shit and the stench had soaked into the material. Rodger drove to the supermarket, he smelt so bad people would retch when he walked past them. One old lady was physically sick right beside him and the manager was called. Rodger moved quickly to the tills as he didn't want to be confronted by the manager, but the cashiers wouldn't serve him, "This till is closed!" One after the other they all did the same thing, he had to go to the self-checkout and do it himself. Every single person around that area separated like the river Jordan, away from him.

"Why the fuck would you come out like that? You dirty bastard!" someone shouted.

"You smell like shit and you look like a piece of shit too!" Rodger ignored him, packed up his shopping paid and left, but the guy wouldn't let it go, he kept on at Rodger. The man got as close as he could stand. "Why don't you crawl back into the sewer that you came out of, you're a dirty piece of shit, look at you! You fucking stink and you think that it's OK to be out like that around people and their families, you dirty bastard."

Rodger had had enough, he let go of the trolley and clenched his fist. "Leave me alone," he told the guy.

"I never knew shit could speak," the man replied, laughing at himself, looking around to see if the crowd, that had now gathered, thought he was as funny as he thought he was.

Rodger's fist clenched even harder. "Say one more thing to me—"

"And you'll do what?" the man laughed again.

Rodger drew his fist back and punched him in the jaw, clean out. No one said a thing as they would have probably done the same to that weasel.

Rodger walked out of the supermarket and loaded his car, everything that had just taken place made him angry. He wanted to go the cemetery, he had to find out where his parents were buried. He wanted to dig them up and kill them all over again and tell them he was living in the house they never wanted him to have, just to laugh in their faces. He blamed them for the person he had turned into, and he felt he had every right to.

He put his head down when he got there as he was sick of the way people would stare at him and if his head was down, he couldn't see the hatred in their faces. It didn't take him long to find the grave of his parents, as it was with all the newly buried. Someone must have visited them as there were freshly planted flowers and the beginnings of a rose bush, also a few vases of lilies and sunflowers and they already had a headstone. Rodger chucked the flowers out and smashed the vases. "I hate you," he cried out, not wanting to shed any tears for his parents and he didn't, he was crying for himself. Everything seemed to have got on top of him today, he wanted to pull them out of the grave but now wasn't the time. He left and got into his car and sped home.

Once in the house he fed the pigs, he was missing Pepper not being in the house but he wasn't going to give in and let her in. "Time to feed myself." He said, rubbing his hands together He chucked some onions and mushrooms in a pan, cut some potatoes up into chips, and chucked them in the fryer. They didn't take long to cook, so he slapped the steak in with the onions and mushrooms, one minute each side, blood seeped out of it when it touched the plate, then on came the chips, and the rest of the veg out of the pan. He ate the meat like he was sucking the flesh out of someone's neck, and the plate was empty within five minutes. He cracked open a can and downed it, opened the second and sat back on the sofa, news on. The lady who he tried to kill a while back was dead. She was so traumatised by what had happened to her she simply couldn't go on; she could think of nothing else only what had happened to her. The smell of Rodger never left her, she took her own life, her family were on the screen, begging for any information. The newsreader asked the family about her, and they said she was such a kind and beautiful person and that she wouldn't hurt a fly but since this happened to her she wouldn't speak to anyone, only repeating the same words, '*the smell*' over and over. She wouldn't eat or sleep, she had lost the will to live, her dog had died on the night she was attacked, this broke her heart as she loved that dog. It was her baby, her children were teenagers and doing their own thing, but her dog was her constant companion and the evening she took her life was actually his birthday. Apparently she went up to the loft and jumped out of the window, falling onto the glass table in the yard. Her family heard the crash from the kitchen and ran outside, but she was dead before the ambulance arrived. She had planned the whole thing.

Author: Rodger why are you not feeling anything for what you did to that lady? You really are a cold-hearted bastard. I will get back to you shortly.

Rodger switched the TV channel, not because he thought what have I done? He didn't give a shit, he turned channels because he had already forgotten about that episode in his life. He didn't care about her or her family and that the pain for them will never go away, he was over it.

Author: I told you I would get back to you, the lady, the one on the news who took her own life, her name was Angie. She had indeed planned the whole thing, in fact she wanted to do this exactly a week after her ordeal. She had left a letter for her family, and it was on the table right in front of them.

To my loving family

I am so sorry I am writing to you about this.

I truly love you all so much and more. My beautiful children, your hearts will hurt so very much for me, and for a while. I am so sorry, I didn't mean to hurt you, I really didn't. I just had to go as what that man did to me took away all hope of ever being normal or happy again. Even with your beautiful faces shown in front of me every day, I could still not see anything but darkness, his hands around my neck and although they were no longer there I could still feel them. The smell of him, so horrific, not one day did that smell leave me, it was like it was in my pores, it was in my nails, it lived in my nostrils. No matter how much I washed, no matter how much perfume I sprayed it was still there. I even considered slicing my nose right off my face but I couldn't because of you two. I am going to go now, but always remember Mummy loves you and always loved you and I will take that love with me. Look after your dad and each other. Forever and eternity, I will wrap my arms around all of you, you may not feel it, but they will be there, love you always, I am so sorry, I will see you when I see you xx

Chapter 9

EASY PEASY

Rodger had turned over the channel again, he couldn't relax, he had to go out and walk off that huge meal, clear his head and have some fun. He knew exactly where he was going, he was going back to the old man's farm, he was easy pickings, as he wasn't going to fight back. The evening had gone by so quickly, it was eleven fifteen, if he started walking now it would take forty-five minutes or so, but first he had to add a few items to his backpack; he knew he was going to kill the old man.

Rodger's heart was pumping so hard, it was the excitement of killing again. He avoided everyone he passed, hiding behind trees, bushes anything he could find until the coast was clear. A couple were walking nearby, but obviously couldn't see him, he made sure of that, he overheard the man say, "Can you smell that? Someone needs to clean up round here." Of course, it was Rodger, his stench lingered in the air, he just couldn't get away from people judging him, whether they could see him or not. He wanted to appear from behind the trees and stab the life out of the couple but he waited until they had drifted off into the distance.

Rodger checked his watch, it was eleven fifty-three, he arrived at the old man's house in just under forty-five minutes, better than what he had thought. The lights were still on, and he was sitting around the dining table again. 'He must be stuck there,' Rodger thought. The old man's hands were shaking hard, Rodger walked round to the front porch, the door was open. "Stupid old twat," he said. "Who the hell leaves the front door open nowadays at this time of night?" He crept into the house, the floorboards creaked beneath him. He could see the old man straight in front of him, he must be deaf as a post because he didn't hear Rodger walking towards him. Rodger continued straight to him.

The old man was startled when he saw Rodger. "Who are you? And what are you doing in my house?" he shouted.

"You left the front door open!" But of course he didn't hear a word Rodger was saying.

"You smell really bad!" the old man retorted.

Well that was like a red rag to a bull. "Shut the fuck up you old bastard!" He taped up the old man's mouth, he didn't move an inch, it was as if he knew it was his time, perhaps Rodger was doing him a favour. The old man's eyes were fixed to the wall in front of him, his hands shaking so much they were making a tapping noise on the table. This infuriated Rodger. He pulled the axe out of his backpack and chopped them off; blood splattered the walls. "Thank fuck for that, no more tapping" he laughed. Blood poured out of the handless limbs. Silence filled the air; the severed hands had rocked to a still on the table. The old man dropped back on the dining room chair. He was dead. It was either the blood loss or the shock of what had just happened. Rodger obviously didn't care, and he couldn't or wouldn't leave it there, he wanted more, after all he didn't walk all that way for nothing. The old man's nose was protruding out from his face and, for the remark he made earlier, it would have been rude not to, so out came the Stanley knife. He put his latex gloves on and began to slice away at the flesh, it was relatively easy, but the bridge of the nose was proving a little harder to detach. Couple that with a dead body that was moving with each slice, so Rodger decided to lay him on the floor. He wiped away the excess blood from the end of the knife so he could see the sharp edge of the blade. He sliced away at the gristle and bone, it didn't take as long as he thought.

"You can't smell fuck all now you old cunt." Packing everything back into his rucksack like a child at the end of school day, Rodger went out of the door as he had come in, not a flinch, leaving the old man dead and bleeding out.

Rodger didn't give two hoots about what had just occurred, but all that not-giving-a-shit attitude was making him sloppy. He had left the nose on the table, it was of utmost importance that he take it with him. He turned back to the house tracing every step done previously to the kitchen, he picked up the severed nose and just put it in his pocket. It would be a treat for pepper.

Rodger looked at the time. He didn't realise how long he had been at the old man's house, it was a couple of hours and the heavens seemed to have opened up while he was there. Thankfully it had eased a little now. He started his journey back home but the rain that had poured earlier was proving to be a problem. It was extremely boggy and slippery in parts, and he continuously got stuck. It took him twice as long to get home. On his way he saw someone walking towards him, so he hid in the bushes, well fell into them, but unbeknown to him at that point, the person had spotted him.

"Are you OK in there?" the man asked. Rodger didn't answer. "Can you hear me? Are you OK? Do you need an ambulance calling?" Still no answer, but he could hear him dialling. This panicked Rodger, so when the guy's back turned slightly, he had no choice, he leapt out of the bushes and grabbed the man in a chokehold. He dragged him into the bushes.

"Why couldn't you just leave well alone? Now I've got to kill you too!" The man fought for his life. This wouldn't be that easy, rolling around the muddy banks exchanging blows. In the fight Rodger's bag had come off and some of his 'tools' were strewn across the ground. He managed to grab the closest thing to him, it was the pair of scissors, and he stabbed away at any part of the man's body. Still he wouldn't give up, he fought for every bit of his life. After a while Rodger proved too strong for him and, with all the stabbings he had received, the strength was leaving his body; he could fight no more. Rodger stabbed him a few more times until he was dead. He got to his feet, out of breath, his clothes heavy from the thick, gloopy mud. He picked up his bag and replaced all of his tools, looking around to check that he was alone and there was no one else to surprise him and he carried on his way home, as if he hadn't just killed a man.

Chapter 10

COKE AND BEER

On his arrival home all the pigs were asleep apart from Pepper. The way she looked at him was as if she was pleading, 'Let me in'. whilst grunting and shivering, and Rodger did just that. That pig was the only thing that loved him, and they went into the house. He put some kindling and logs on the fire and stoked it up. The house was soon nice and toasty. Pepper lay in front of the fireplace, and Rodger gave her the old man's nose and threw a towel over her as she was shivering. With one bite it was gone and after a short while she fell asleep. Rodger had to now sort himself out as he was cold, soaking wet and covered in mud. He took off all his clothes right where he stood...

Author: I wonder if he will put those clothes in the wash? Who am I kidding of course he won't, does he even have a washing machine? If there was one, he'll probably never use it.

He ventured up the stairs, slipping halfway up on Pepper's shit, left previously, twisting his ankle. The pain was excruciating, but he managed to drag himself up to his parents' room, where he was looking for something to put on. He found his dad's pjs and an old dressing gown, he struggled putting them on for a few minutes as he couldn't stand for long as his ankle pained him but he continued to get dressed sitting on the floor. "Pepper you fucking prick! Now look what you've made me do." Of course, Pepper was fast asleep, Rodger shuffled down the stairs, avoiding the shit, on his backside easing his way down each step. As he got to the bottom he held onto the banister and hoisted himself up. Putting his foot to the ground he winched in pain, mumbling, "This is all I need."

Author: No Rodger, what you need is a bath! Get a grip, you've twisted your ankle, the way you keep telling us all about what you've been through, a twisted ankle should be a piece of piss, just get the hell up and stop moaning.

He got to the fridge grabbed four beers, and sat on the rickety sofa, whisky already on the table beside him. He took a huge gulp, then cracked a can and that went straight down. Looking at Pepper in front of him, he couldn't stay mad at her, she was the only thing that loved him. She didn't care how he looked or smelt she just loved him, but she was just a pig. Drinking the rest of his beers he felt a little more relaxed, he continued sipping on the whiskey too. He couldn't feel the pain in his ankle any more. Hunger soon took over so over to the fridge he went, he wanted something quick and easy. "Eggs and bread, perfect!" He cracked his eggs into a pan and chucked in the bread, within minutes it was ready, so with his tea of fried bread and eggs, not forgetting a couple more cans, he headed back to the rickety sofa. Pepper's snout pricked up, she smelt the food, this of course woke her up. Rodger had made plenty so he scraped some on the floor beside her, and they both wolfed it down.

Rodger was really knackered but he fought that sleep as he knew all the nightmares would enter his mind. Trying everything he could to stay awake, he paced the living room, pinched himself, watched TV, but nothing worked. Then he remembered, he had a bag of cocaine in his backpack, he had taken it from Wesley's place, and had totally forgotten about it. "That'll do," he said. He searched the trousers he had not long taken off, still in a wet and muddy mess on the floor, for his wallet and found a five-pound note. He rolled it up and lined up some of the cocaine into two neat lines and snorted one after the other up each nostril. After fifteen minutes, Rodger was absolutely fucked. He had only tried it a few times in his youth, and had forgotten the feeling of coke being mixed with too much alcohol and that it wasn't a good combo. He felt sick, the only bonus was being wide awake, and that was probably a good thing right now.

Chapter 11

PC JOHN BLAKE

PC John Blake was absolutely devastated and heartbroken for the lady and especially for her family. It had always been his dream to be in the force but the devastation he was saw in people's eyes after the traumas they were going through, meant he was at breaking point. He needed to solve this case, he promised the family wholeheartedly that he would find whoever was responsible for doing this to her. He went into work and searched through every single criminal record that had any similarities to this case. This would take him weeks but this he had to do to solve it.

He worked from morning till night, the piles never seemed to get any smaller, yet he soldiered on. This, of course, made his home life miserable, and the few hours he did see his wife and children was taking its toll on his family. Arguments would override the deep love he had for them but nothing mattered. He had to solve this case. He even had a heart attack scare as he was drinking copious amounts of Brandy to get him through.

One evening after going through more records, he sat back with a loud sigh. He buried his head into hands wondering if he would ever be able to do this, then suddenly, he remembered Rodger, and only because of him smelling so bad. He went to the chief superintendent to tell him about it.

"What evidence have you got on him John?" was the reply he got. He tried to explain but he was so shattered that the words simply wouldn't come out. "Go home and write a statement, you are in no fit state to share anything right now," the superintendent told him.

John went home. Once there, he was greeted to emptiness, his wife had packed up and left with the children. He rang around everyone he could think of to find out where she was, eventually he found her whereabouts; she had gone to her estranged father's house.

"It's either me and the children or your job John!" she shouted down the phone to him.

He chose his job, he explained again, that he must solve this case. "I need to find peace for that family, Georgina."

"What about your own family?" she asked.

"I'm sorry, darling, I promise after this case I will leave the force, please, please just trust me and give me one last chance, I won't let you down," he pleaded. "You and the kids are my world, but I need to do this."

"I can't promise you anything right now, I need to get my head straight and I will talk to you in a few days." And with that she put the phone down.

John Blake poured a glass of Martell and began writing his statement for the chief. It detailed how he went round to Rodger's house to give him the news of his parents, that they had crashed their car as a result of his mum passing out behind the wheel. This then caused a pile-up that killed a family, and left a lorry driver in a critical condition, and still in a coma. But most important was the stench of Rodger, he smelt so bad that he and the other attending officer couldn't go into the property on one of the last visits. Also he mentioned how cold Rodger was, saying how he didn't care that his parents had died. All of these things never left John, but he had no evidence against him, so his file just went on the pile.

The next morning arrived so quickly, he had fallen asleep on the statement he was meant to show the chief, but he had no time to rewrite it. So a dribble and a brandy-stained statement would have to do. He jumped in the shower and wet shaved his face, cutting into the flesh. To stop the bleeding he ripped little pieces of toilet paper and stuck them on the cuts and got dressed. Once at work he was ready to see the chief only to find he wasn't there yet. This gave him chance to pull out Rodger's file. He read through it and was happy to see that he had mentioned about the stench of Rodger and his home before; he was hoping this would be some sort of evidence.

When the chief arrived he had totally forgotten he had told John to write his statement, that didn't sit well with him at all. John was pissed but he was determined to see him. He sat out outside his office for ages until the chief's secretary reminded the chief John was waiting to see him. John finally presented his statement to him, but the chief wasn't impressed with what John had to offer at all. "Please let me go and question him Chief, what do we have to lose?" he pleaded.

After a while of back and forth between them, the chief let up and let him, but he needed to take another officer with him, so John and the officer with whom he had first gone with went to go and quiz Rodger.

They pulled up to his old house, but of course Rodger didn't live there any more, there was no answer. This really annoyed John off, as he thought Rodger was in and just ignoring them. "If he's not here then where could he be?" the other officer piped up. "Why don't we try his parents' house? It's worth a try and we have their address from before."

John wasn't happy about this, one, because he didn't think of that and two, because this was his lead, he wanted to solve the case so badly for that poor family but letting his pride get in the way and to not be undermined he said, "No we will sit and wait until nightfall, he's going to have to put some lights on and maybe venture out."

Night fell and nothing happened, no lights, no twitching of the curtains, nothing. They decided to call it quits for the night, so they went back to the station. John didn't bother to go in, he got straight into his car and drove home. He was so annoyed with himself, he knew she was right but he didn't want her to be, he wanted the glory for himself.

The next morning, they did exactly what they should have done the day before and went to Rodger's parents' house. Knocking on the door, there was no answer. Rodger could hear them but he never answered the door to anyone.

"It's the police! Open the door!" John shouted.

Rodger froze. "Shit! Shit! Shit!" he said to himself. "What should I do?"

"If you don't answer, we will knock it down!" John continued. This was just a scare tactic, he knew he couldn't do this as they didn't have a warrant. It worked.

Rodger opened the door "What do you want?" he asked.

"We want you to come down to the station, we just want to ask you a few questions, about an incident that occurred not too long ago, involving a lady who was attacked." That very smell that had engulfed John and his partner's noses the first time, was ten times worse now.

At this point Rodger was dying inside. 'Fuck! They know it was me, I can't go back to prison,' he thought.

Every bad thought went through his head, so much so that he had a panic attack in the back of the police car. As they arrived at the station, Rodger had calmed down, he had to. In the interview room they began to question him.

"Where were you on the night in question?" John asked.

"I was at home."

"Can anyone back you up on that?"

"No, I was on my own with Pepper," Rodger said

"Who is pepper?" the female officer chimed in.

"My pig," Rodger exclaimed.

Sniggers came from the officers, but Rodger's face had no expression. Sweat started to drip from his forehead. "Why are you sweating?" John quizzed.

"It's hot in here," Rodger replied simply.

After questioning Rodger for the majority of the day and to no avail, they had to let him go. There was no evidence to say that he was involved.

Rodger was relieved, so much so he asked the question, "Can you take me home please?"

PC John Blake did just that. Once outside Rodger's house, John turned to Rodger and told him, "I know it was you that attacked that lady and I will be watching you."

Rodger, getting out the car, looked at John and with a smile, just before closing the car door said, "Prove it."

Chapter 12

A LOT MORE COKE AND BEER

Rodger knew he had had a lucky escape and was feeling slightly confident but still he stayed in that smelly farmhouse for days on end, just in case they were watching. He continued to snort coke and drink alcohol to counteract each other, trying to forget whilst trying to remember. Trying to block out the voices so he could sleep but wanting to stay awake. Eventually he couldn't fight the sleep any longer, but as soon as he shut his eyes, his head rattled, he heard every voice that did him wrong and the voices mixed up into one. He could feel every time he was raped and sodomised over and over again. His mother's voice grated on him. All of the destruction, everything he had ever suffered, was there haunting him. He tried and tried to wake himself but it was as if everything that happened gripped his eyes together. They were not going to let him wake up, they wanted him to feel everything over and over again. He was fighting and having none of it. Still in his nightmares, he tried turning the tables to how he wished his life to have been, growing up was not as he lived it, it was his twin brother not him. Rodger was the one who got the most sweets, the most hugs, and all the attention. He was the one who passed Joe bread and drinks in the understairs cupboard. Joe was the one that was raped and sodomised by his cell mates. Their parents loved Rodger more, his brother didn't steal his girl. It was the other way round.

Sadly for Rodger reality came back with a thud. "Don't be so stupid, we will always be here in your head and we will tighten that grip every time you dare to fall asleep. We will forever haunt you, we know you can hear us and feel us. You're so stupid. You're a dumb ass, we will forever enter your dreams and your every thought."

He would hear his mother. "You're weak! You're a dirty boy Rodger and I hate you!" She was laughing but not in a nice way, more like an evil witch.

With every strength he could muster Rodger woke himself up, it was light out, his heart pumped so hard he could almost see it protruding out of his chest; the cocaine and alcohol didn't help either. He wanted to hurt someone, anyone, but of course it was only him and Pepper, and he couldn't hurt her. So he began beating himself up, punching himself in the face. "You're useless!" he shouted. He picked up the whisky bottle, finished it then proceeded to hit himself with it. It hurt like hell but he continued talking to himself. "I can't even love me, why the fuck would anyone else." He kept hitting himself again and again. Looking at the reflection in the window he was totally ashamed of himself and how weak he really was. Then it clicked, everyone he came across saw it and now he saw what they saw. He of course blamed his mother, the hate that he had for her was pitted in the bottom of his gut. "Fuck it," he said, with another snort of coke. *Ping*. His eyes opened up like saucers, it took away the pain on every level. Rodger shouted, "I'll show you who's weak."

He was going to go on a shopping spree at midnight or thereafter, he would kill and torture whoever crossed his path. The ones he planned to

kill, some were out of prison now and the others that were still in would have to wait. Rodger didn't have a clue how to find the ones who had been released, but they would get hell when he did. Wesley was found by a pure stroke of luck, well for Rodger obviously not for Wesley. But unbeknown to Rodger, his next killing would be sooner than he thought.

His next victim came straight to him.

Chapter 13

GOD SERVING PEOPLE

There was a knock on the door and, because he was coked up he had let his guard down, he opened it, something he would never normally do. He only realised his mistake when it was too late. It was the God squad, a woman and a child.

"Do you have time to talk about our Lord and Saviour? May we come in?" the lady asked.

"Why? What do you want?" Rodger snapped.

"We have just come to spread our good Lord's work," the woman said happily. His eyes veered to the little girl, she looked like an angel. Her eyes were as blue as the sky, her hair was red like a burning flame but his eyes were drawn away from her when asked again, "Can we come in, sir?"

"The name's Rodger, not sir!"

"Hello Rodger," she answered holding out her hand to shake his.

The little girl whispered to the woman, "It smells in there," whilst pointing in the house,

"Shhh! Don't be so rude, that's what we are here for, to help, if it's needed and to spread the good Lord's work, now say you're sorry to him."

"But, Mum, it does, it does." The lady apologised for the little girl.

"It's OK, that's kids for ya, come on in," Rodger said with a smile. When the little girl saw Pepper she was a little scared but Rodger assured her Pepper wouldn't hurt her and that she was friendly. "Go and sit with her, if you want," he told her.

As they entered the house they shuffled around all the shit and rubbish. "My name is Catherine and this is my daughter, Mary, she is four years old." She then babbled on and on about God, and how, "He will not desert you in your time of need."

"He has deserted me all my life," Rodger answered back. "My whole life has been utter shit from the day I was born."

"That's not God's fault," she said.

At that point, Rodger started to zone out, her lips were still moving but he couldn't hear any sound. He was imagining how he would kill this gobshite and which part of her body he would slice off first. 'Her lips and tongue would be first,' he thought.

She must have been talking for at least half an hour, but somehow he coerced her into the kitchen. Once in there he grabbed her by the throat and squeezed as hard as he could, her eyes opened wide and filled with tears, Rodger held his finger to her mouth for her to keep quiet, he then stuffed a dirty rag in her mouth, from the kitchen side and taped it up. He got her to stand on a chair and hold her arms up so he could tie her hands to the pipe that ran along the ceiling. He pulled the stepladder out from behind the door, climbed up and tied her hands tight around the hot pipe, he then tied her legs together at the ankle and tied them to it too. She hung there, hog tied, like meat hanging out to dry, a look of sheer terror in her eyes. He got close to her, pulled up her dress and smelt her inner thigh, of course he couldn't do anything as Mary was in the other room and he was still pretty high from the coke, so he returned to the living room. The little girl was unaware of what had just happened, and she was happily playing with Pepper.

"Mary, your mum has popped out and she has asked me to take you home," Rodger said with a gentle smile. Mary just looked up at him and asked if she could stay and play with Pepper a bit longer. "Of course you can!" he told her. "Just for a little while though." He couldn't resist those big blue eyes. He went to the kitchen, had another line of coke and grabbed a beer out of the fridge, then he sat on the rickety sofa and watched Mary play with Pepper. It was nice to hear genuine laughter, he hadn't heard that since his relationship with Jane, the one his brother had stolen from him. 'He stole the only laughter and joy I had,' he thought to himself. It was nice to hear it once again. If only he could keep her, he knew it wouldn't be possible, how would he look after a little girl? He couldn't even look after himself.

Rodger closed his eyes for only a second only to be startled by the loudest scream he had ever heard. He jumped off the rickety sofa only to see Mary looking up at her mummy. That was the last thing he wanted her to see, but thought that it was a good job there were no neighbours close by, she screamed so much she made herself sick.

"Mummy! Mummy, wake up! Wake up, Mummy!" Mary continued to scream.

Catherine managed to open her eyes, a single tear rolled down her face, she knew she couldn't help her daughter. Her eyes gazed upon Rodger, it was a look of, 'Please don't hurt my little girl.'

Mary wouldn't stop screaming and shouting. "I want my mummy!"

Rodger had no choice, he grabbed some gloves, his balaclava and scraped his dirty clothes on, he got the car keys out of Catherine's bag, and bundled little Mary into the car. She screamed so loudly, thank God no one could hear apart from maybe her mother who now couldn't do anything. Mary was still screaming, with every ounce of strength she had in her little body. Rodger wasn't used to noise, as well as the laughter, it was just him, Pepper and the dark of the night when he ventured out. this had become his way of life, he shouted over her screams. "Shut the fuck up or I will kill you!" With that her mouth slammed shut, he didn't mean to frighten her, he just wanted her to shut up. From the moment he had met that little girl he saw an angel staring up at him, it never even crossed his mind that he would harm a hair on her head. He drove thirty miles out and told her to get out, but she started whimpering.

"I want my mummy." He had to physically chuck her out of the car hoping that no one had seen him. He knew she would be found as he dropped her close to a hospital, and there were a few people about. Hurting or killing children was not on his agenda, although he did just that by taking her away from her mother. That little girl will be traumatised for the rest of her life.

Driving back home he stuck to the speed limits, he didn't want to draw attention to himself. he got back to the house and remembered he wasn't in his own car. "Maybe that's a good thing, if I was spotted they will think Catherine was driving the car." He knew her car had to be put in the garage, it was a ball ache though, as he had to move his to put hers in. He would think of how to get rid of it later.

Going into the house he could hear her whimpering. As he entered the kitchen he looked at her, the skin on her wrists as melting to the pipeand her ankles were almost sizzling. He filled a pot of cold water and chucked it over her. "That will cool you down!" He then paced back and forth for a while thinking, 'What the fuck am I going to do with her?' He couldn't believe he wrecked little Mary's life, he snorted another line of coke and punched himself in the head. "What the fuck have I done? Why did I hurt these people? They were nice to me they wanted to help me, what the fuck have

I done?" His mother's voice poured into his thoughts. "She's now in my head while I am awake how is she doing this?" he said sounding scared.

"They didn't care about you, who the hell would want to help you? You are such a loser!" his mother was telling him. He put his hands over his ears.

"Leave me alone you fucking bitch! Just leave me alone!"

Rodger reached for a beer and another line of coke, something that had now become the norm, he continued pacing his shit and urine-soaked floor. "What should I do with her?" he asked himself over and over again. The more he paced the floor, the more the smell of shit and piss rose into the air, but he couldn't smell a thing as he was used to his surroundings and completely at ease with it. A sharp pain climbed up from his ankle but with all the coke and alcohol, he just braved through. Little Mary was his main concern at the moment, he hoped she was found and was safe. He was so scared and racked with guilt that he never waited to see if she was found. Another line of coke made him feel better, ending Wesley's life was a double bonus as if it wasn't for his stash he probably would have killed himself but he also knew this wouldn't last forever, he had to find a dealer and soon. Saying that, he had at least another two weeks' worth but with the amount he was using it wouldn't last that long.

Author: For crying out loud you really are pathetic, I am so glad you have finally seen a glimpse of how weak you really are and how everyone else sees you! What took you so long? Killing and torturing people doesn't make you strong. Get a grip and sort yourself out! Have you forgotten you have a woman in your kitchen tied up to a blazing hot pipe? Throwing cold water over her will not stop the pain, it will probably make it worse. You said she was nice to you, so if that's how you treat someone that's nice then God help us all.

Chapter 14

DON'T TALK ON THE PHONE

Rodger headed for the door, it was eleven forty-five p.m. It was like it was programmed in him, the beer and coke seemed to give him an inner strength. He walked over the hills, and it wasn't long before he found his next victim, some cocky young lad in sunglasses at night. 'Who the fuck wears sunglasses at night?' Rodger thought, that alone infuriated him.

The lad dared to say something. "Fucking idiot, ha ha."

Big mistake, Rodger got in his face, put his hands either side of his head and snapped his neck, simple as that. As the young lad fell to the ground his phone dropped out of his hand; there was a voice on the line. "Sam, you OK? What's going on Sam? Sam, you OK? Who is that with you?" Rodger hadn't realised that the young lad was on his phone, he wasn't directing anything at him at all, he was talking to someone else. So this young lad, who now lay dead on the floor, was simply killed for talking on his phone. Rodger didn't have an ounce of guilt, he picked up the phone and ended the call, took the sim card out disposed of it, put the phone in his pocket and carried on like nothing had happened. All the walking was taking its toll on his ankle but the pain he felt wouldn't stop him. He dared to venture from those fields and muddy hills, the street lights in the distance drew him. He was getting brave and feeling untouchable, there were a few people about but far and wide from each other or so he thought.

He glimpsed a woman all on her own, so, creeping up behind her, he dragged her into an alley way. Her perfume engulfed his nostrils, and it turned him on, a feeling he hadn't felt since the lady and her dog. He had to be inside her but what he didn't yet know was that she was in fact a he and a person of the night. She attempted to scream, so Rodger put his hands around her mouth and slammed her hard into the ground. He sat on her with his full weight, she could barely breathe, one hand remained on her mouth while the other reached into her underwear. He was taken aback when he felt her penis. "What the fuck?" he said surprised, but it didn't stop him from wanting to nail her. He flipped her over and did what he had to do. After he had done his deed he slammed her head against the concrete path a few times, either trying to kill her or knock her out he wasn't entirely sure. Either way he pulled his clothes up and attempted to walk off, but as he appeared at the opening of the alley there were two guys looking for her. One the guys shone a light down the alley, saw her lying there not moving.

They shouted over to Rodger, "What have you done?"

"What do you mean?" Rodger asked. "I just went for a piss, I don't know what you're on about." Of course they didn't believe him, they both rushed him, tackling him to the ground. Rodger landed with a thud. Fists rained down on his face, neck and chest, full force kicks to his body, one of them stamped on groin, he howled in pain. They beat him to a pulp, his ribs were broken, his nose was bloodied and he had a massive gash to the back of his head. He couldn't take any more, he did try and fight back but these guys were too strong and there was two of them. He had to think fast, he had to get away, but not before they removed his balaclava. His face was so battered and bruised, he got back on to his feet trying to get away, but they kept pulling him back, punching and kicking him to the ground.

One of the guys said, "Give me the torch, I need to go and check Tootsie." That was Rodger's chance to get away. He pulled together the last bit of strength he had for the punch the guy, that was still on top of him, was about to receive. Rodger clipped him a good one right on his jaw, the guy fell backwards all bent up. Rodger pushed the rest of his body off of him, got to his feet and legged it, ignoring the pain that roared through his body.

As he reached the fields, he wished he had never left those muddy banks and shielding bushes, so he sat for a while to compose himself while hugging his broken ribs. "This is it, my game is up, those guys saw my face, I will be going back to jail for sure if I get caught," he told himself. The thought of going through what he had experienced, the year he had already spent in prison, would be too much, he would rather kill himself than go back there. Arriving back home he bent down to the fridge to grab some beers. "Shit! Shit! Shit!" he said aloud. "They've got me now, how could I have been so stupid to even consider going down there." As he straightened himself up from the fridge, which he had to do slowly because of his ribs, he nearly pissed himself, he had also forgotten he had Catherine tied up above him to the hot pipes, the smell of her burning flesh the only thing that reminded him, so he cut her down although every move felt like another rib was being broken. He stopped for a minute, went into his backpack, got out the duct tape, lifted his top and proceeded to wrap the tape around his torso as tightly as he could. His painkiller would be, of course, his cocaine and beer as he couldn't go to the doctors as he did not have one and the hospital was out of the question.

He went back to Catherine, she was quite clearly dead, he remove all her clothes. She was as hot as hell, her blood must have boiled inside or she had had a heart attack from the shock, either way she was gone. He took a few minutes to look at her naked body but he felt nothing. Getting a sharp knife and his axe, he sliced and chopped her into several pieces, like an experienced butcher with a carcass. The pigs could smell her blood. He did consider burying her as she was so nice to him, but he was in too much pain with his ribs and head, however, no matter what he had to move the pieces of her body. He dragged her across the floor on a plastic sheet, stopping every two steps to catch his breath. He got to the door, opened the pig pen and pulled her in. How he managed it he did not know, she was just as heavy in pieces. The pigs soon surrounded her body and feasted.

Hobbling back into the house, blood now joined his cesspool of a home. He was now on his last few beers, and he had to think how he would get some more but for now he would make do, and with the cocaine plus the few bottles of sherry and wine his parents had left behind he should be OK. He spotted Catherine's bag and rifled through it, inside he found her purse, it contained some cash and a few bank cards., "I could order some beers on her Mastercard.' He thought but he had to be clever and order it to another address. he searched in her bag to see if he could find her address. He struck gold, her address was on a letter she had left in her bag, it would be smart to send it there as it was her card after all. He also ordered some food and bandages as well, plus a toy for little Mary, she would never get it but it made his order seem more realistic and fitting for Catherine, so then if it was checked, there would be less suspicion… He gave a specific time for the next day, he would be waiting outside her in the morning, which was practically here as it was now five twenty-four a.m. He really, really hated going out in the day, but needs must.

Surprisingly she didn't live too far away, maybe a fifteen-minute drive, and it was a farmhouse with no neighbours like himself. Those few hours seemed like forever.

Rodger got there before the delivery, sitting in the car slumped as low down as he possibly could, hoping no one would spot him if they should walk or drive by. It was excruciating but the beers would be worth it. He could see the delivery driver arriving so he waited for him to unload the items, he then knocked at the door, obviously no one was there, he posted card through the letterbox and got back in his van and drove off, as soon as he did Rodger was ready. He pulled his car right up to the house and loaded it up, putting a pack of beer in the front seat, it took him no more than two minutes. The boot was full, and he got back in the driver's seat and drove off. It was very near miss though, as he looked in his rear-view mirror there was a swarm of police cars pulling in at her house. They must have found little Mary. He put his foot down, he wasn't seen, well he hoped he wasn't. He cracked one of those beers as he drove back home, then another, he needed it for his pain, well that's what he would tell himself anyway. Back home he just chucked everything in the kitchen and went back to his rickety sofa, fetching beers as and when he needed them. Rodger realised he had bigger fish to fry. Those guys in the alley, had seen his face, but did they get a proper look? He put the news on to see if anything had been reported and there it was all over the news. There was a description of him but he wasn't a, 'Man of colour' as they described, it was just dirt and so much of it. Dirt filled his beard, his hair was almost black with filth, shit and God knows what else. He looked in the broken mirror. Looking back at him was someone Rodger didn't recognise, his voice was the same, and his eyes were the same, but nothing else.

Author: I wonder if this will now make you take a bath and clean yourself up because if you don't I will not be able to write a sequel, you have so much more to do. I know you won't let the bastards who really hurt you get away from the wrath you seek to put upon them. You're not finished with your mother either although she is dead.

Chapter 15

TIME FOR CHANGE

Rodger knew what he had to do, he had to clean himself up. The smell, the dirt this is what would catch him out. He tried washing his face in the kitchen sink but it was filled with pot and pans and he couldn't get into it, also he couldn't bend, so he went upstairs. Every step jarred at his broken body but he got there, he ran a bath and threw the soap in that he had found in the cabinet. His clothes fell to the floor with a loud thud, they were so heavy with filth. He took off the tape that bound his body, that was painful, it pulled hair at every he had. The bath was now filled and he had months' worth of filth to remove, all he had to do now was step into it. He hadn't done this in such a long time but the time was definitely now. He got into the water, it was so hot yet he didn't feel the heat as his body was so thick with dirt. He literally had to scrape off the layers, at first all seemed impossible so he just lay back and let his body soak so the soap and hot water could do its job, the same way you would leave a pot or pan to soak after cooking. After ten minutes the water was brown with floating debris, so he emptied the bath and then filled it again, this time rubbing the soap through his matted hair. That was a task on its own. Sinking in the bath the same as the last, he must have changed that bath water five times before he could see the soap instead of searching for it. He washed his hair several times, face too, he decided to shave his beard but would wait until he came out of the bath. He was so relaxed and felt a release from all that weight he was carrying around, plus his ribs didn't hurt as much while he was soaking. One more water change and it was as clear as his white skin, his hair was a mousey brown as was his beard. After relaxing those hours away he got out of the bath and chucked his clothes in the water. The water immediately turned a different colour, and he soon realised he shouldn't have bothered as they were ready for the bin anyway.

Rodger was a very dashing man. He stared at himself for a while and thought about how he looked. "You're not bad looking there, kid," he said. He had just never seen it because his mother clouded every goodness he ever had, he never felt worthy. Now out the bath, he had to find a clean towel but to no avail, so he just drip dried while he cut away at his beard so he could then shave it. It took him a while as it was extremely long and very thick he then used a random toothbrush out the pot to clean his teeth, he couldn't see how good he really looked because of course, he had broken all the mirrors and the biggest piece was downstairs or so he thought.

I Rodger and Joe's childhood room, which then became just Joe's room still contained all of things including stuff from when they were children. Pepper didn't venture into his room as it was always shut, to be honest the most mess she had made up here was on the landing. He entered the huge wardrobe in Joe's room, it was full of good clothes and shoes, and on the door was a full-length mirror. He looked around and realised everything he needed for this new chapter was in that room. "but Why did Mum keep all his stuff from when we were kids and not mine?" he quizzed, as if he really needed to ask. He put some jeans on, no boxers as he wanted to feel free, a nice shirt, that hugged his body, black socks and brown shoes, he put the comb through his hair then a splash of aftershave. Although he was still in really bad pain and bloody knackered as he hadn't slept properly for such a long time, which was the worst bit for him, he felt good, though he was afraid of being shunned, as he had been every time he went out. But he knew he had to do it, so never minding the consequences and putting one foot out of the door then the other, he felt great in all his get up.

The first person who saw him didn't blink an eye, or shun him, instead he got a friendly smile. He arrived at the village pub but waited outside for a while, plucking up the courage to go in. He saw a few people going in and out, they looked at him but again didn't blink an eye, this gave Rodger the green light to enter. He walked straight to the bar, and asked the barmaid what she would recommend. It was one of the special beers, new in. She kept staring at Rodger and he thought, 'Here we go again'. But he couldn't have been further from the truth, she was actually looking at him, as though she found him attractive. She was one of those girls that was quite forward but not in a slutty way. She worked in a village pub that was full of older frumpy men, and Rodger was a pleasant sight to see and extremely easy on the eye.

They exchanged names. "I know you didn't ask for it but my name's Sandra," she said with a smile. "How about you tell me yours?"

Rodger went bright red and with a shy smile said, "It's Rodger." And with that they were introduced, they talked for the whole night. Rodger really liked her, maybe she would be the one to make him really happy. She asked him about his life and if he had any family, and he obviously lied. He changed everything about his life, he made it sound perfect. His mum and dad were still alive, his brother was his best friend and how he used to be in the troops but now he works from home with a very successful business, something to do with finances. All these lies would come back to haunt him eventually but for now it didn't matter. They talked some more and he asked her about her life and her interests. Before he knew it, it was closing time, and he had to go.

"Will you be back tomorrow?" Sandra asked.

"Yes it's a possibility." He didn't want to come across as desperate. "Can I give you a call in the morning to let you know, as I may have to work." Another lie, she passed him her number. As Rodger made his way home, he was happy, happy in a way he couldn't remember feeling or if he had ever felt. The walk home seemed to be quicker than the walk there, his head filled with positive thoughts. Tomorrow couldn't come quickly enough.

Once home Rodger wasn't tired like he had been for so long, he had so much positive energy he was buzzing with this new-found feeling. He couldn't sit down, he couldn't wait to hear her voice so he called her, it was really late though so he wasn't sure if she would answer, but she did, as soon as she answered the phone.

"Hi, it's Rodger just to let you know I have cleared my schedule, so if it's still OK I can meet you tomorrow, say about seven p.m., oh and sorry I called you this late." He didn't give her time to speak but Sandra didn't mind at all, she sounded as excited as he was. They talked on the phone for quite a while until she told him she needed to go to bed.

The second meeting was pretty much like the first, they talked more about each other's families and their upbringings. Rodger's family sounded like an absolute dream. A mother who cherished him and his brother, taking them out on day trips, playing fun games in the house, and always there for them both. His father, a hardworking man who made sure he and his brother were brought up with morals and a hard work ethic, showing them how to love and respect women as much as he did their mother. They got on like a house on fire and Rodger felt as though this was the start of something special. He felt that, for the first time in his life, someone understood him, and liked him for him but it wasn't the real him it was who he wanted to be. But even though he had told these lies about himself and his life, everything else was real, his personality, his sense of humour it all came through the very night he met her. The true him was now coming alive, and as long as they got on and he was happy, everything else could stay buried deep for now.

Chapter 16

FAIRY TALES

Over the next few weeks their relationship flourished. Rodger was beside himself with happiness, but he always had that niggling feeling in the back of his mind that something or someone was going to fuck it up for him, but only time would tell. The one thing that put a damper in their relationship, was that he would never take her to his place, which made Sandra think he was hiding something. It was purely the state of the house, but she thought that maybe he had a wife at home.

"Why can't we go to your place tonight?" Sandra asked, "I've told you before, it's a mess, I'm having work done."

"And I've told you I don't care about that, what are you hiding?"

"I'm not hiding anything, as soon as it's done we can go to mine, I promise." Rodger always reassured her and told her that she never had to feel insecure, he wanted to be with her. He knew he couldn't go on like this especially if he wanted to keep her in his life so he decided there and then to do something about his living arrangements.

Saturday soon approached, and Rodger decided that today was the day, he rose quite early, meeting Sandra had kept his mind calm so he was sleeping at night only for a few hours but it had become routine now, it was a beautiful sunny morning, he put Pepper back in the pen with the other pigs, and he scraped up all the shit that littered his home for the longest time. This was going to take him hours as most of the debris and filth was dried to the floor. He threw out that rickety sofa, which he got so comfortable with but it had to go, in fact everything in that living room had to go, there was no saving anything. He piled it all up outside away from the pig pen and started a fire, even the clothes he tried to wash were thrown on and any of the other filthy clothes he had worn time and time again. The amount of beer cans strewn around the house was immense, it took him aback. "What the hell have I been doing with my life?" he asked himself. Whisky bottles and other half empty bottles everywhere, he was disgusted. Once he had got rid of all these bits, he started to see the wood through the trees, but that was just one room, he had the kitchen and all upstairs to do. It took him just over a week to clear everything out, now for him to go and get some cleaning products, he would need a crateful of bleach and plug-ins, as that smell wasn't going anywhere fast. Rodger was doing this for Sandra, he couldn't lose her. Everything was in working order in the kitchen, he even found the washing machine. It still had his mother's clothes in it, they were chucked on the burn pile. He was still only dealing with cash so all the furniture he needed, he got from Ikea, it was the easiest and cheapest option, the house would be ready soon.

Rodger decided to call on Sandra to see if she would like to go out for a bit of fresh air and a spot of food. "Yes, I know the perfect place, we can go for a walk, it's so peaceful and the scenery is beautiful." Sandra said, always happy to spend time with him.

"Sound," he said. They decided to meet at the pub, it was one p.m. and it was a lovely day. They had a few drinks first, his ribs still pained him not as bad as before but they twinged every now and again, but he knew a couple of whiskies would help with that. Rodger had got the pub a little earlier to collect one of their picnic baskets for them to take on their walk. He went up to the bar to collect it, it was filled with champagne, strawberries, and some beautifully prepared sandwiches and cakes. "So where are you taking me Sandra?"

Unbeknown to him, she was taking passed some of the spots he had killed and attempted to kill a couple of his victims. As they drew nearer, they passed by the very place he strangled that woman, *'the smell'* one. He could now see it, like it was on repeat, he could see the woman's face so clearly, this freaked him out. That wouldn't be all, as they carried on walking, he saw the young lad, the one on the phone, and the other guy, the one he killed for trying to help him. It all appeared in front of his eyes. Haunting him.

"We will come back for you, you're never going to be happy! Why did you take my life? You will regret it. I am going to be with you wherever you go! You will suffer as we did!" This was swirling round his head like bees round honey, their voices so clear, he was as white as a sheet.

Sandra noticed. "What's up? Are you OK babe?" Of course, he couldn't tell her, but she then said something that knocked him for six. "Is it because of all the attacks and murders that have happened round here? Well, I'm not afraid because I am with you." She carried on talking. "Only someone who is born evil could have done what that person or people have done, did you see it on the news? They killed two people and tried to kill some woman but she died from the trauma he had caused. I hope they catch him or them soon, they need to be put in prison and left for the other inmates to do what they need to do. They should be fair game like the ones he killed! Do you think it was the same person? Can you imagine living with yourself after that? Like how do you look at family or partner and act normal? It's crazy!"

Rodger had heard enough. "Shut the fuck up! Just stop fucking talking!" He suddenly stopped and just looked at her, realising what he had just said, but it was too late. He was horrified. 'That's the old Rodger talking that's not me, or am I just a sheep in wolf's clothing?' he thought, his mind racing.

"What did you say to me?" she asked, clearly shocked. The old Rodger appeared for a second and he regretted it instantly. He was in a trance-like state. "Rodger! I said what did you say to me?" This time her voice was raised.

He answered her. "Oh my God, Sandra, I didn't mean to talk to you in that way at all. I really don't know what came over me. I'm sorry." But he did know, he knew exactly where that came from. "I am so sorry Sandra," he continued in a calm voice. "Do you mind if we go somewhere else? This place freaks me out."

Sandra seemed to accept his apology. "It's OK, we don't need to talk about it right now but don't talk to me lie that ever again." She looked at Rodger as he nodded in agreement. "come on let's go it's starting to freak me out too. You choose where, next." She continued, grabbing his hand as she led them away.

Rodger knew in that moment that no matter the fairy tales he had spun to her about his life, that's all it was. A fairy tale.